This book belongs to:

Once upon a time will you . . . meet a pri
Baby Bear? Will you make friends with F
from trees? Or see a snail with a saddle? `
you have a water fight, help Little Red H
count the rats following the piper? Will
land? Will you fly on a carpet or zoom or
telescope? Or through the magnifying g
behind a tree? Will you find magical trea
you, live in a hut on an island by yoursel
a map, find a magic lantern, see the sn
look out for the great growly bear, or w
seas on a pirate ship, play croquet, ride c
fearsome fox, ask the magic mirror a qu
Will you eat curds-and-whey crisps? Will
your rags into a ballgown, disco dance w

ce, outwit a **crocodile**, or play music with

ss in **Boots**? Will you find **icicles** hanging

ill you make the **wicked fairy** cross? Will

n make **bread**, ride a **dancing unicorn**, or

ou step through a **wardrobe** into another

broom? What will you see through your

ass? Will you spot a **sneaky wolf** hiding

ire? Will you take a **hot-water bottle** with

dance with a **duckling**, kiss a **frog**, follow

es on the **trees**, find an **ostrich** to ride,

e a **magic wand**? Will you sail the seven

a **swan**, or trick an **ogre**? Will you find a

stion, or choose to live in a **shoe house**?

ou spot a **small cricket**, magically change

a **tin soldier**, or defeat the **evil wizard**?

*For the wonderful charity Home-Start that pairs trained
volunteers with young families in need of some help*

P.G.

For all those who have shared their battered You Choose books with me

N.S.

PUFFIN BOOKS

UK | USA | Canada | Ireland | Australia | India | New Zealand | South Africa

Puffin Books is part of the Penguin Random House group of companies
whose addresses can be found at global.penguinrandomhouse.com.

www.penguin.co.uk   www.puffin.co.uk   www.ladybird.co.uk

Penguin
Random House
UK

First published 2020
This paperback edition published 2021

004

Text copyright © Pippa Goodhart, 2020
Illustrations copyright © Nick Sharratt, 2020
The moral right of the author and illustrator has been asserted
Printed in China

The authorized representative in the EEA is Penguin Random House Ireland,
Morrison Chambers, 32 Nassau Street, Dublin D02 YH68

A CIP catalogue record for this book is available from the British Library

ISBN: 978-0-241-48887-4

All correspondence to:
Puffin Books, Penguin Random House Children's
One Embassy Gardens, 8 Viaduct Gardens, London SW11 7BW

MIX
Paper from
responsible sources
FSC
www.fsc.org   FSC® C018179

YOU
CHOOSE
FAIRY TALES

In a fairy tale, who would you choose to be?

I'm happy as long as nobody kisses me!

Look at the pictures and choose your own story.

Nick Sharratt & Pippa Goodhart

PUFFIN

Welcome to your fairy tale in a land far, far away.

What kind of hero
will you choose to be today?

Which of these fairy-tale homes would suit you?

A castle? A cottage?
A very big shoe?

What will you be good at in this story we are making?

Running? Dancing? Sword-fighting? Or baking?

Every story hero needs at least one loyal friend.

Choose your true companions to be with you to the end.

You're off on an adventure!
The signposts point the way.

Take a road to somewhere new. Where will you go today?

How will you travel
to where you want to go?

Time to stop and have some lunch. What will you choose to eat?

What items might be handy as you go about your quest?

Stop! There's danger up ahead – including giant feet!

Which of these baddies would you least like to meet?

What might happen next? There's so much you could do!

Will there be magic or mischief?
The choice is up to you!

There's a ball at the palace!
The band will sing and play.

Who will you choose to boogie with as you dance the night away?

Your adventure's nearly over.
You're snuggled up in bed.

Choose a bedtime story,
or make one up instead . . .

Did you make it through that **maze**? Or c

you extinguish a **fiery dragon**, swim with

best friend, or go to the **witch hat towe**

you have a **sword fight**, find **four** and

dormouse in a **teapot**, or ride in a stretc

of **angry sisters**? Did you find the **house**

lion, or drink from the **bottle** that said

fiendish moustache to wear, or watch yo

the **scowly slithery snake**? Did you choose

a **small deer peeping**, or tightrope walk o

house, ride in a **pumpkin coach**, pick fr

wearing a 'G'? Did you run as fast as a gi

give **Tom Thumb** a ride in your pocket, o

the **terrible troll**? Did you live in a h

shoemaker elves flying? Or a **frog eatin**

Did you build a little **brick house** with

unt how many dwarves wore purple? Did
flippy fish tail, have a butterfly as your
Did you spy the green-eyed spider? Did
venty blackbirds baked in a pie, spot a
limousine? Did you keep out of the way
nder the bridge? Did you hug a friendly
rink me'? Did you feed the birds, find a
nose grow long? Did you watch out for
live in a tent or a teapot? Did you notice
a braid of hair? Did you live in a crooked
toffee-apple trees, or notice a character
gerbread man? Did you find a glass shoe,
fly away on balloons? Did you creep past
use made of sweets? Did you spot two
a pea, or Pinocchio in his new clothes?
big? And did you live happily ever after?

YOU CHOOSE

Nick Sharratt   Pippa Goodhart

A NEW STORY EVERY TIME – what will YOU CHOOSE?

OVER 1 MILLION YOU CHOOSE BOOKS SOLD

YOU CHOOSE YOUR DREAMS

Nick Sharratt   Pippa Goodhart

A NEW STORY EVERY TIME – what will YOU CHOOSE?

OVER 1 MILLION YOU CHOOSE BOOKS SOLD

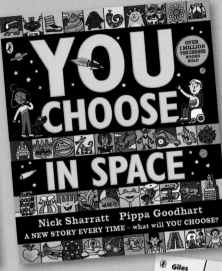

YOU CHOOSE IN SPACE

Nick Sharratt   Pippa Goodhart

A NEW STORY EVERY TIME – what will YOU CHOOSE?

OVER 1 MILLION YOU CHOOSE BOOKS SOLD

Giles Andreae   Nick Sharratt

Pants

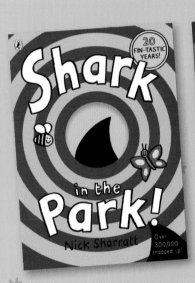

20 FIN-TASTIC YEARS!

Shark in the Park!

Nick Sharratt

Over 300,000 snapped up!

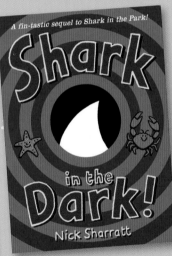

A fin-tastic sequel to Shark in the Park!

Shark in the Dark!

Nick Sharratt

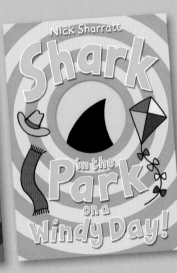

Nick Sharratt

Shark in the Park on a Windy Day!

Giles Andreae   Nick Sharratt

Animal Pants

Giles Andreae   Nick Sharratt

Party Pants

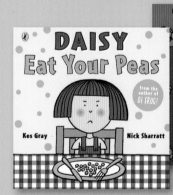

DAISY Eat Your Peas

Kes Gray   Nick Sharratt

from the author of DI TROG!

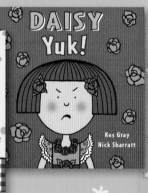

DAISY Yuk!

Kes Gray   Nick Sharratt

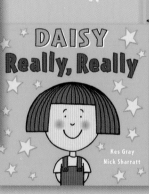

DAISY Really, Really

Kes Gray   Nick Sharratt

DAISY Tiger Ways

Kes Gray   Nick Sharratt

DAISY 006 and a Bit

Nick Sharratt

DAISY You Do!

Kes Gray   Nick Sharratt

Why not choose some more books illustrated by Nick Sharratt?